Where Do Dragons Poop?

POEMS AND PICTURES BY
RINKART NIGHTHAWK

This book is the first of three books in the Mythical Poop Book Series. Also look for "Doo Genies Need to Poop?" and "Doo Zombies Poop in Public?"

A green dragon knows when it's time to go—

it has to stop wreaking its havoc below.

It has to stop screeching and bellowing flame,

it has to stop smashing and playing its game.

A green dragon knows pooping out in plain sight

is worse than the arrows or dizzying height.

It flies off to find a nice quiet commode,

a place to relax, to unwind and unload.

Because a green dragon understands this whole thing,

it brings along TP so the poop doesn't cling.

She's beautiful, strong, and has the purest white glow
but despite all the glamor she still has to go.
When saving a maiden or prancing around
she calls a timeout and just poops on the ground.

Eunice Unicorn

It doesn't smell lovely, and for certain not sweet,
   but watching her poop is to see beauty excrete.
The reason you haven't seen all this before
   is there isn't a unicorn living next door. Sorry.

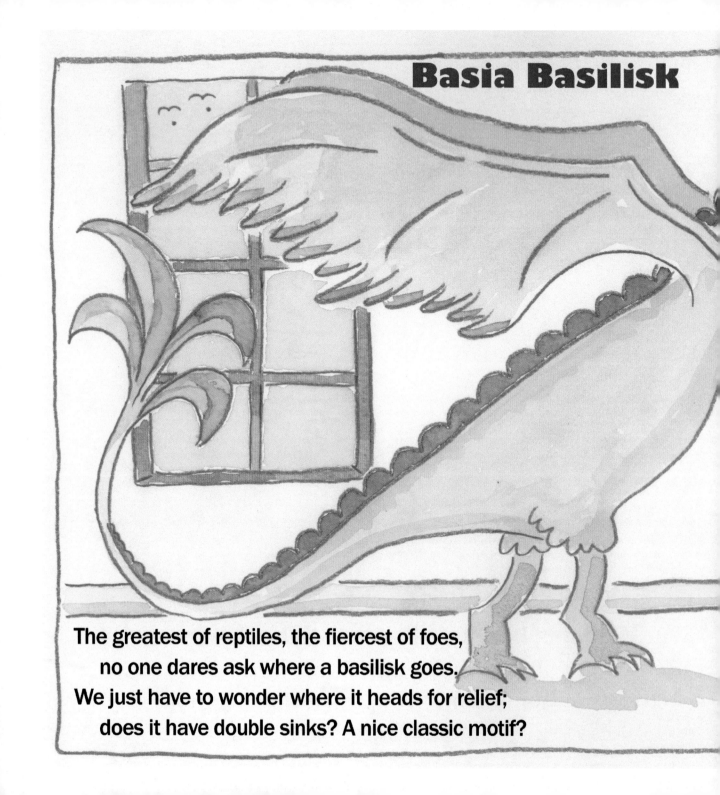

Basia Basilisk

The greatest of reptiles, the fiercest of foes,
no one dares ask where a basilisk goes.
We just have to wonder where it heads for relief;
does it have double sinks? A nice classic motif?

An elongated toilet,
  eco-friendly, and white?
A nice, warm bidet spurting
  just the right height?

If all of the legends we've heard are our guide,
  this bathroom will not have a mirror inside:
If a basilisk sees its reflection at all,
  it becomes a stone fixture inside of the stall.

Blake Black

It shouldn't be a joke because the subject's just not funny;
   black dragons tend to wait too long, then poop comes out all runny.
Instead of fearful dragon fire coming out its mouth,
   it's killer jets of dragon squirts a-coming out down south.

And even though it's only diarrhea coming out,
   that poop is just as deadly as the fire from its snout!
Black dragons are embarrassed when they're having tummy grief,
   and never leave their dragon throne till they have found relief.

Kraig Kraken

Much like your goldfish that swims in a tank,

a kraken just swims in and breathes his own rank.

He lets loose his bowels in a bubbly flurry,

and ships going by open sail in a hurry.

A kraken is mean and his power is super,

but he's just a regular, mythical pooper.

If threatened someday by this ocean wrongdoer,

just chuckle and point, then say, "Back to your sewer!"

Peggy Pegasus

Oh where, oh where does a pegasus poop?
  Oh where, oh where does she go?
Like a bird she flies in a wide loopty-loop,
  then drops her biscuits below!
The plop and patter of turds on the car
  seems like the end of the world.
But because the poop's from a rare flying horse,
  it's fine whether scattered or hurled.

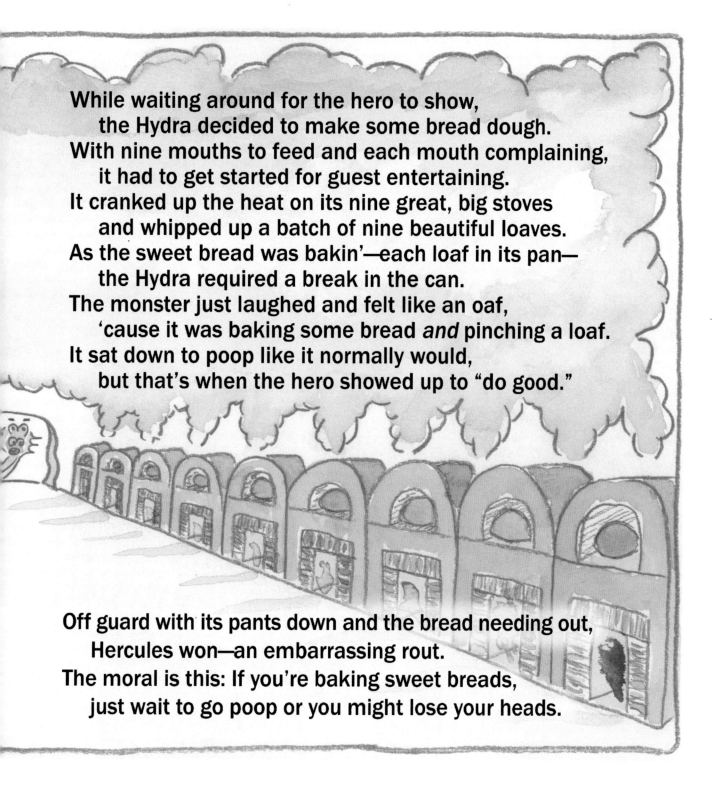

While waiting around for the hero to show,
    the Hydra decided to make some bread dough.
With nine mouths to feed and each mouth complaining,
    it had to get started for guest entertaining.
It cranked up the heat on its nine great, big stoves
    and whipped up a batch of nine beautiful loaves.
As the sweet bread was bakin'—each loaf in its pan—
    the Hydra required a break in the can.
The monster just laughed and felt like an oaf,
    'cause it was baking some bread *and* pinching a loaf.
It sat down to poop like it normally would,
    but that's when the hero showed up to "do good."

Off guard with its pants down and the bread needing out,
    Hercules won—an embarrassing rout.
The moral is this: If you're baking sweet breads,
    just wait to go poop or you might lose your heads.

Phelix Phoenix

Its beautiful feathers burn yellow and red;
   this smoldering Phoenix just rose from the dead.
But even the newly arisen must poop,
   so Phelix ducks in through a pyramid stoop.

He struts and he squats in the Phoenix restroom,
and finally leaves "something" in somebody's tomb.
How long will it last? Will the foul smell endure?
Of course! After all, it is Phoenix manure.

Nessie Loch Ness

In faraway Scotland, in a lake known as Ness,
a rarely-seen monster is making a mess.

Like all mythic creatures she must daily poop,
whether all by herself or in a large group.

To think Messy Nessie's alone in the lake
would be, as they say, a stinking mistake.

Nessie's whole family, along with fish schools,
  just swim there together through poopy fish stools.

If someday you see Nessie rise from the water,
  it's a privacy thing: she's a world-famous squatter.

Red dragons love to gather gold and put it in a heap.
They lay there on the shiny pile until they fall asleep.

There's nothing in the world that makes a dragon leave its guard,
except a call from nature when its poop it must discard.

It growls and bellows fire when it has to leave its post,
but pooping on the treasure is what dragons hate the most!

It finds the dragon bathroom three tunnels on the right,
and quickly goes, then wipes its hiney just to be polite.

It races back to find the hoard, the treasure, and the gold,
but squeals as it lays back on top, 'cause now the pile's cold.

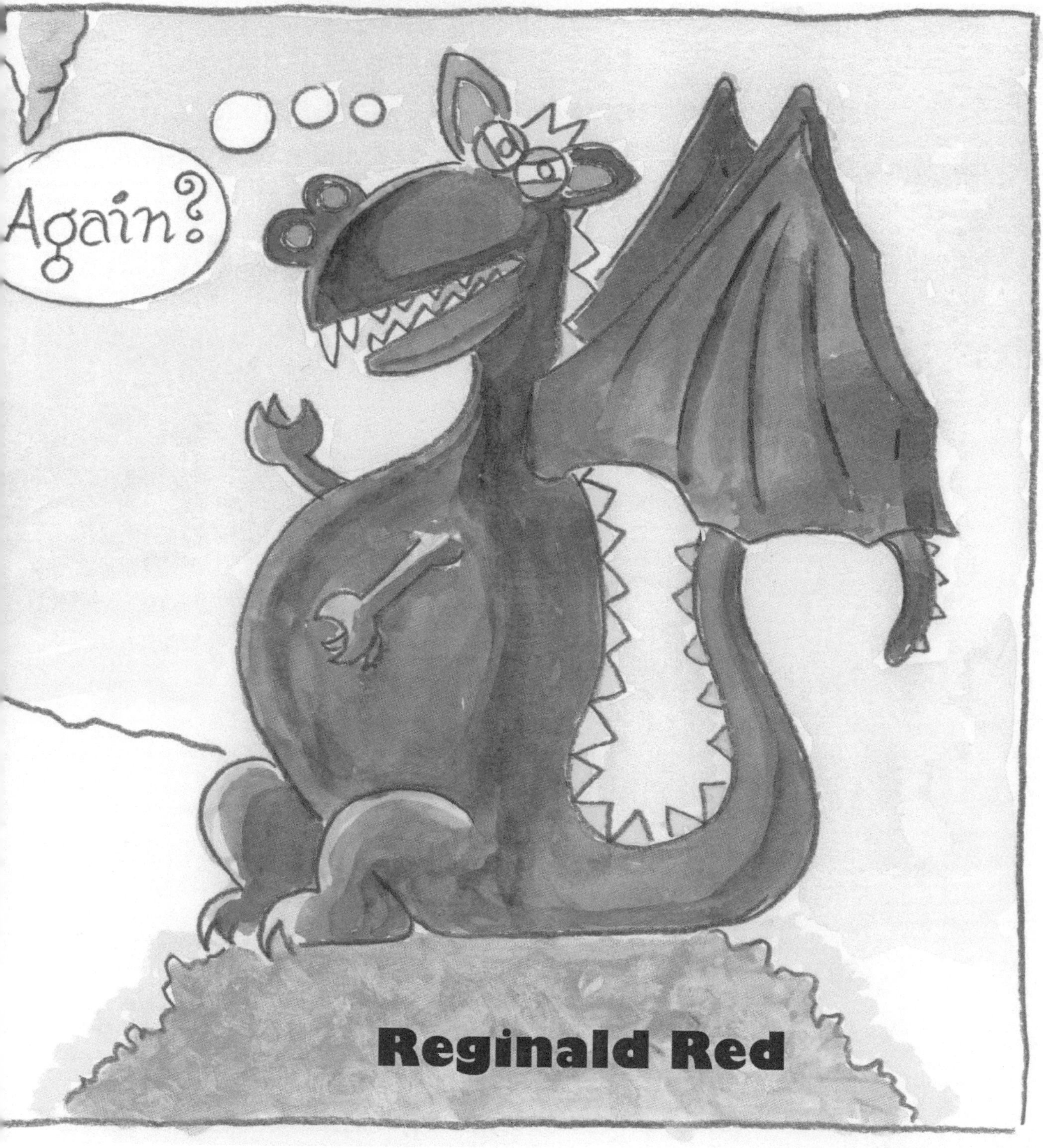

Reginald Red

And where all that poo goes is somewhat foregone:
that somewhere just happens to be the back lawn.
Would you be the one in charge who picks up
the triple-sized dog logs from a three-headed pup?

Be happy that you get to use just a bag
for your little-sized, one-headed dog
"Colonel Flagg."

If you had the three-headed monster out
back, you'd find yourself picking up
poop by the stack!

Gordon Golden

The fiercest dragons ever found
  are golden-colored and renowned
For eating every little bit
  of every meal, yes every whit.

So what was it that dragons ate that
  made them clean their dragon plate?
Do they like sweets and party feasts?
  Or do they snack on woodland beasts?

The answer may surprise you now:
  it's not a horse or sheep or cow.
It's sure to cause no little frights—
  they love to eat the brave, sir knights

They eat the big knights and the small, they eat the short knights and the tall.
  The dragons gold eat every knight: courageous, handsome or polite.
Gold dragons don't just eat the knight, but everything within its sight!
  They eat the sword, they eat the shield, they eat the spear and armor steeled.

So now the question you may ask—"What about the pooping task?
  "If golden dragons eat knight's gear, won't that hurt coming out its rear?"

Don't fret much about our friend or if he gets it in the end
  From eating spears and knives and bows, 'cause here's the secret no one knows:
Because a dragon belches fire and breathes a hot and gaseous pyre,
  His insides melt the steely lot, and it's a smooth go on the pot.

Welcome to
INDONESIA
Home to the World's
LARGEST LIZARD
REAL DRAGON POOP!

Kory Komodo

The other dragons in this book were just pretend, but take a look!

The dragon you see down below is really real, and not for show.

Komodo dragons walk around and look for food there on the ground:

pigs and deer and buffalo, or smaller dragons yet to grow. (Ohhh...)

Like living creatures all o'er the earth, Komodos poop for all they're worth.

A runny mess with yucky lumps comes gushing out their lizard rumps.

At ten feet long and 300 pounds, avoid the place where they abound!

ABOUT THE AUTHOR

RINKART NIGHTHAWK

Rinkart was raised on a farm and knows poop. The end.

Look for the other two books in the Mythical Poop Book Series:
Doo Genies Need to Poop?
& Doo Zombies Poop in Public?

Made in the USA
Middletown, DE
03 May 2021